2011

JULIO LEANS AGAINST a lamppost yards from where the rest sit, on a bench at the city busy stop. On the bench, beneath an awning, are two women and one man, the latter of whom keeps lifting the left sleeve of his suit jacket and sighing at the dial of his designer watch. As each woman takes their turn staring at Julio, they move their hands as if what's between their fingers isn't a purse strap, but a rosary. Twice now the petite blonde woman has stared and wondered if offering her seat to the child that has elected to stand in the rain would be the decent thing to do. While the heavy woman on the opposite end of the bench has only contemplated it once, of the two, she, ten minutes prior, was the closest to acting upon the thought, struggling to stand and plopping back down once the sound of the bench's relief and the stares of her fellow public transiters forced her face to an anxious shade of red.

Needless to say, for the fifteen minutes they've all been waiting, none of the three adults have spoken to Julio. No one has asked why at 10:30am on a Tuesday, he is here, and not in the back row of Ms. Guiterrez's sixth grade classroom, watching her squiggle the finer details of the Battle of Fredericksburg on the blackboard. He does fidget his hands every so often, as if he has yet to determine where they feel most comfortable: in his pants pockets, or when squeezing the straps of his tattered grey and scarlet backpack. A winter inside has rendered his skin even paler than normal.

"You got that way from your father," his mother has told him before, as recently as Saturday, her Bajío dialect heavy as she broke open the steroid capsules and dumped their powder into the formula already sloshing around the giant metal bowl. "'Go outside for once, northerner, get some sun,' I'd tell him. Light-skinned bastard."

As he has for the past two days—as he tends to do with the few things his mother does say to him—Julio tumbles those words through his skull. Chin to crown, jaw to jaw, they bounce, and lag, like a glitching game of Pong with no goals or paddles, the only endpoint being an interruption such as the approaching bus. Its brakes wince its presence, its approach, its promise of Point A to Point B. The accordion connector wheezes hydraulic pressure into the air.

The man in the suit hurries to the opening door, the two women just steps behind. An automated voice says something a trailing Julio cannot discern. But he walks, eyes, neck, shoulders, everything turned left: a peculiar sidestep rather than a natural gait. His brother's old, soaked shoes squish as he ascends the stairs. He drops in his pocketful of change after the heavy woman does so. Just as he is reaching for the ticket the fare box spits out, the bus driver, a tattooed white man of about fifty, grips his wrist and says:

"Hold up." With his free hand, the driver reaches for the capless Coke bottle from his cup holder and deposits into it one more gob of tobacco spit. He works his dip around his gums and bottom lip, spits once more, then returns his gaze to Julio. "Where you headed?"

"A field trip," Julio says.

"A field trip, huh, all by yourself?" The driver watches Julio nod. "Turn a bit, boy," he says, "no, to the right."

Julio hears a gasp from one of the passengers in the front seat of the bus—either the black woman head-to-toe in white, or from the white girl with caked black lipstick—and understands that it is no use. Despite what they see, none of them will stop this. None will interject. None will rise and unhand Julio from the bus driver.

When Julio does turn, the driver's eyes grow wide at what he sees. Julio's cheek has swollen to double the size of his right; he can open his left eye no wider than a pinky nail; there is a scabbing gash in the center, yellow and purple bruises orbiting. The driver loosens his grip, but does not let go.

"Jesus Christ, kid," he says.

"Can we get this thing moving already?" the man in the suit says from the seat closest to the middle door of the bus, the seat best suited for his imminent leap onto the sidewalk nearest his destination.

The bus driver ignores the man in the suit. He finally lets go of Julio's wrist. "Well," he says, "how'd it happen?" There is a kindness to his voice now, a softness.

And Julio is taken aback by this. He cares not where this kindness is stemming from—whether the driver is a father, a brother, a cousin or uncle—but only that it is there, and that it makes him feel good. Worried for. Needed. It makes him think of his older brother, Oscar, and how, if he were to return home and see Julio's wounds, how the compassionate side of him, once the majority, would ask questions just like this.

"My mother," Julio says, "she hit me in the face with a crowbar."

"Oh," the driver says. The kindness doesn't fade, but it does take on a new shape, evolves from something soft into something lumpy, somewhere between curiosity and knowledge. Like he has seen this before. Like he is conjuring images of Julio being punished for dealing weed, for stealing a quarter pound of sliced ham from the butcher, for spitting in a young lady's hair.

"Drive the fucking bus, would you?" the man in the suit says.

The driver looks back. He grabs his Coke bottle, spits, then swivels into driving position. Before easing the bus into motion, the driver looks at Julio and says, "I guess that'll teach you."

Julio's mother taps the pup's left shoulder with the curved end of the crowbar. The pup—a black and white pitbull with sad cerulean eyes—turns slightly, slacked chain dragging across his already-bulging shoulders, then bites the steel, and cringes before letting go entirely.

"See," Giuseppe says. He stands feet behind Julio's mother, next to Lance, a white man from east of Richmond who'd stopped at an ATM on the way to add to the already-fat wallet resting crooked in his back pocket. He watches the dogs. Over the incessant growling, he strains to hear Giuseppe. Whether or not he hears Giuseppe, whether or not he's on the same page, he nods.

"See," Giuseppe repeats. He straightens his slouch; he folds his arms; he widens his white-sneakered feet; he briefly juts his small, goateed chin: all mannerisms he is certain project confidence. "The steel keeps them in line."

"Wouldn't wood do the same thing?" Lance asks. He watches the pup leap onto his sister's back and gouge her ears with his teeth. She yelps. Together, chains and all, they tumble into the makeshift border between doublewides—satellite dishes, taped together milk jugs, the occasional action figure and plastic fire truck with its hose and ladder snapped off.

"No. No wood. Their jaws become so strong that they bite through. Like kiwi to us." Giuseppe nudges Julio's mother and tells her in Spanish to break the siblings up. It is the first time they've touched in weeks, and Giuseppe couldn't care less. "Watch this," he tells Lance.

Wearing her TACOS HERMANAS work shirt and a pair of knee-high rubber boots, Julio's mother sidesteps through piles of shit and links of chain the pups have already worked off and left to shimmer like gems peeking out of the lawn. Her fake pink nails have been removed, as have the earrings she wore to the market this morning. Yet eyeliner and cover-up remain. A front jean pocket is slightly bulged by her balled hairnet. And she handles the crowbar like a poor, exhausted woman would: with haste, with urgency, shoving the point between the two pups and prying them apart. The boy, having learned moments before that he cannot defeat the object, leaps to his feet. He even backpedals a bit while his sister sees for herself what the steel has to offer. She gnaws on it; she stumbles elsewhere.

"You have to think of the steel as an extension of your arm," Giuseppe tells Lance. "You want them to think—you need them to think—that you are indestructible. That you cannot be fucked with. That you are alpha." Only now does Giuseppe look Lance in the eye. Only now does Giuseppe rub his face with his scarred right hand. Because Lance is no different than the others. A prospective buyer needs to see that the breeder himself is, and has been, a fighter, that he has stabbed and that he has been stabbed, that it's this mentality that will have trickled down to the dogs before him.

But Lance does not look, not for a second. He strokes the entirety of his thick moustache with his index finger. "Can I tell you the truth, Gio?"

"Of course."

Julio's mother walks back to the two men, in the center of her front yard, wishing that, somewhere throughout her nine years in America she'd mastered English. She has tried, several times, and has picked up tidbits here and there—slang, idioms—when she hasn't been seasoning beef and chicken, or mopping floors, or serving hot lunch to charter school misfits. But rules. Hard Ks, Gs that sound like Js, I before E. Rules. Rules. Rules. Too many rules, and too many teachers saying too many different things in too many different tones to navigate. Too many men like Lance chasing more money when they already drive decked-out Silverados down potholed roads and into weed-and-thistle driveways expecting the desperate to not key the tinted windows, or pawn the upgraded exhaust. She wishes she knew English because she doesn't want Lance to fit this projection. She wants the truck to be a façade. She wants him to purchase the last two of this litter. To award Giuseppe enough money to leave on his own, without confrontation, enough to wander and latch onto the next puta he can trick into giving him her coño. She thinks she wants out of this neighborhood, out of Richmond, out of this doublewide. But that isn't true. She wants out of her skin but has not an idea whom else's she would rather inhabit.

"Well," Lance says. He adjusts the sweat-stained ball cap atop his balding head. "The truth is that none of 'em look like fighters. Not a one. Except for her." Lance points at the pups' mother, who stands erect in the shady corner of the yard, snarling, as she has been doing since Lance's arrival. A thick chain digs into her scarred neck and shoulders. A fly bites at her jagged right ear. "She looks like she could take down a lion."

"She could," Giuseppe says. "As vicious as they come." He puts his right hand on Lance's shoulder. "But she didn't get that way overnight. I can promise you that." Giuseppe, after easing his confident posture into something calm, proceeds to tell Lance what he has been telling men like Lance for a year now, that Lucina, that vicious bitch in the shade saved his wretched life.

###

THE LEGEND OF LUCINA

(paraphrased from Giuseppe's account)

From the moment Lucia and her five siblings were born, to the moment they each were sold, never would she or they drag heavy chains through the lawn. Never would they be deprived of their mother. Never would they attack their siblings' throats over a steroid-sprinkled formula. No. The six played. The six ate. The six pooped. And the six slept. That was all. That was enough. Because Giuseppe's Uncle Fabian didn't raise fighters. He housed dogs. Until they were of age to be without their mother, and could therefore be sold for hundreds of dollars, he showed generations of pit bulls love, and family.

As for what happened to those loved pups after they were sold, Fabian didn't care to know. All sales were final. And not just, "don't contact me if something goes wrong" final, but more like, "I don't ever want to see your face again" final. Anyone that knew of Fabian and his dogs knew the story of Fat Ricky, a neighborhood hustler who'd refused to take Fabian's rules seriously. Weeks after he'd purchased a dog from Fabian, and fought that dog without rest on three separate occasions, Fat Ricky approached Fabian on foot as he was parking his truck at a gas station and shouted, "You sold me a fucking chump! Nothing but a fucking chump!" The truck had barely stopped moving before Fabian leapt out from the driver's seat and put Fat Ricky—a man who outweighed Fabian by eighty pounds—in a chokehold. Hours later, Fast Ricky would have a bucket of water dumped on his face by the gas station attendant, sit up, and realize that Fabian had stripped him of his clothes and dragged him into the middle of the road.

Why Fabian kept as much distance as he could between what he did with the dogs and what they did with the dogs was simple: he had too weak of a stomach; he was too weepy of a man. From time to time, despite exerting no effort to do so, he'd catch wind of results. Of wins. Of losses. Of wads of cash in cold, ruthless hands. Of bloodied heaps of bone and muscle and heart and love.

Yet, year in, year out, he sold them. It wasn't the only way for a part-time janitor living in a trailer to make ends meet, but it was the only way for a part-time janitor living in a trailer to preserve hope. To put any sort of money away, in an account. To send any money home, to the family members he'd left behind. To have the power to stay, and the power to go.

With Lucina's litter, in particular, by the time buyers came around, poor Lucina had come down with a cold Fabian didn't have the time or know-how to treat. She moved with a lethargy that evoked phrases like, "She won't make it a year," and, "That's all you have to offer?" Nobody wanted her. Nobody wanted her then-narrow shoulders, her then-miniature paws, her then-dry nose and then-exposed ribs.

To Fabian's surprise, at the same time his bitch became pregnant again the health of passed over Lucina rebounded. Because with the trailer, space was always an issue, Lucina became an unannounced gift to his nephew, Giuseppe. He knew that Giuseppe and his girlfriend, Olga, had been fracturing for months. Over jobs, over drink, over the slog life demands. Without something new, without something hopeful, Fabian figured they wouldn't last past winter.

He waited until early one morning when he knew Giuseppe and Olga would be home. And, in the cage she would soon outgrow, Lucina cried for Fabian as he slid back into his station wagon and backed out of the driveway.

"The only chance at reviving the relationship is through common ground," Fabian told Giuseppe over the phone, hours after Lucina was discovered and brought inside. "Through something small, and cute, and in need of love—from both of you."

Lucina continued to cry, off and on for days, when Giuseppe would leave for job interviews and return with not only a bruised ego, but with pocketfuls of rum shooters he used Olga's money to purchase. Only when he would let Lucina out of the cage and onto his chest would the crying stop. She'd lick his face, his fingers, his chin, and, though it in no way made Giuseppe's struggles vanish entirely, it helped. It helped him focus not on what he couldn't do, how he was failing, or what he actually could achieve in this country, but the impact he, if given the chance, could make on the life of something. It helped him remember that legacy doesn't start and end with employment.

It helped up until the moments when Olga—a chesty, trilingual (Spanish, Portuguese, English) secretary for a tobacco farmer named Evans—would come home, walk into the living room, interrogate what she desperately hoped was her soon-to-be groom, and, in discovering the day's (lack of) results, lob harsh, linguistically-tangled slurs his way. To which Giuseppe would sit, and listen, and rub Lucina's soft white ears. The one time Olga slapped Giuseppe during the climax of such a scenario, Lucina nipped Olga's hand. Blood surfaced. And when Olga, her rage transferred to

Lucina, reared back for another slap, it was Giuseppe who swatted her hand away.

Later that night, after Olga strayed to another man's hand, Giuseppe brought Lucina into he and Olga's bed and said to her, "I have your back, too."

Within a week, Olga changed the locks and a jobless Giuseppe and a growing Lucina were living with cousins, with old friends, with any other San Salvadorian who'd made their way to Richmond but found themselves in a slightly better situation. They slept on porches, in driveways, and on sofas that had been set on curbs for garbage men to hoist into the backs of their trucks. She lived off of restaurant scraps, and rats she either found hobbled or already dead. He lived off of twenty-five-cent cracker packs, and rum. Their persistence despite the conditions, Giuseppe thought, could only stem from the anger that comes from being unwanted.

One night, on a Main St. bench, when he couldn't take it anymore, Giuseppe held Lucina close and cried into her shoulder. He said no words. He sang no hymn of sorrow. He cried. He sobbed, and she let him.

Another night, Giuseppe, tiptoeing toward blackout drunk, plopped down by a rosebush in Monroe Park and passed out. He still can't recollect what he dreamt of, or how long he actually slept, but he did wake, and when he did, Lucina, standing next to him, was growling. Fierce. Vicious. Tones he'd never heard before. Giuseppe sat up to see the large silhouette of what he'd know moments later, when lying limp, was an eighty-pound German Shepherd. In an instant, without glancing at Giuseppe, Lucina leapt forward and tossed her adolescent paws at the Shepherd's face as if they were fists. The dogs rose on their back legs, a gap between them filled by night sky and dew-covered grass. They growled. They bit. They danced. And it all made Giuseppe ache. A hundred needles jabbed into his heart.

He rose to his feet as tufts of fur floated to the ground, and increased his pace from a walk to a jog when the Shepherd bit down on the tip of Lucina's left ear. What happened next halted Giuseppe entirely: how instead of letting the pain steer her, Lucina let the Shepherd take the ear. She let the Shepherd tear a chunk of the thing off—a sacrifice for position. She yanked free, cranked her neck, and sunk her teeth into the Shepherd's exposed throat. The Shepherd yelped and Lucina clamped her teeth tighter. She held. And held, until moments later the Shepherd bled out.

"This is my last dime, Uncle," Giuseppe said into the payphone's receiver the next day. "My last one. I need advice, not judgment."

"Advice for this moment, or the next?"

Giuseppe looked at Lucina, fur still bloodied a day after her first kill. Starving. Wounded, but satisfied, and standing tall. "Does it matter?"

Fabian sighed, then said, "Use that dime to feed her. Then, I guess if you're telling me the truth—that you don't have any other goddamn option—you fight her."

"Uncle," Giuseppe said, "but it killed me to see what I saw, to see the teethmarks on her cheeks." They were deep. It was painful for Lucina to chew. "I just can't."

"Don't fight her then, what do I care? What do I know?"

"Uncle, don't be like that."

"Don't be like you," Fabian said. "Use your head for a second. Just one fucking second.

Understand that you're too stupid to make money off of yourself. Understand that she's more valuable than you'll ever be. Understand that she's—" Fabian continued.

Giuseppe was no longer listening. He was envisioning what was to come: a day later, Lucina would win her first official fight. And ten days later another. Within months, he'd have enough for a rotation of males.

"Now, think of that pedigree," Giuseppe now tells Lance. "You've heard of Makhai? And Segomos?"

"Hers?" Lance asks. "Makhai is hers? Jesus. I watched him rip the jaw off some terrier last month."

Giuseppe turns briefly at the wincing of the city bus's brakes behind him. He watches Julio descend the bus steps with the straps of his faded grey and scarlet backpack over his shoulders, his brother's old, ratty Adidas sneakers looking as if they'll fall apart with any of his next five steps.

"Just think of what these little ones will be able to do for you," Giuseppe says. He points at the pups. "Think of the money they will put in your pocket."

"How do you explain that then?" Lance asks. He watches Julio's mother, crowbar still in hand, scratch Lucina's neck. Her tail doesn't wag, but the growling has stopped. She even lifts her chin ever so slightly, inviting longer strokes.

"Outside of me, she's the only one she'll let touch her," Giuseppe says. As Julio merges from the sidewalk onto the lawn, Giuseppe notices a folded sheet of paper in the boy's hand. With his free hand, Julio waves at Giuseppe, to which Giuseppe nods, surprised but pleased that the boy is intelligent enough to understand an interruption greater than that would be unwelcome at this time. "Let's go inside, Lance, and discuss how you'll be training them."

Lance nods and, with Giuseppe, walks across the lawn and up the two green-carpeted steps leading into the doublewide.

Julio stops feet from the puppies' chained reach and watches his mother stroke Lucina's ears. He wishes he didn't feel a twitch of jealousy whenever he sees this scene beneath the magnolia tree. He remembers leaping with Oscar from root to root. He remembers the two of them failing to clamber up the trunk. He remembers the two of them pounding thick nails on the northwest side so that they would have a route to the lowest-hanging branch, several shelves on which to place their feet.

He still loves that tree. And he still loves this house. He still loves the woman whose name is on the mortgage, but who has allowed everything to slip through her fingers.

Loneliness," Oscar had said so many times, on so many nights, he and Julio up well past midnight, trying within the four walls they shared with one another to figure out why their mother could possibly want to stay with Giuseppe. "There's no other option. Loneliness has to be the driving force. Don't you think, Julio?"

Julio had nodded. Oscar was older, Oscar was smarter. There was no reason to question that what he'd observed had merit. But after a moment, Julio said, "Or fear."

"What do you mean?"

"I don't know."

"No, what do you mean, Julio?"

Julio shrugged his shoulders. "Maybe she's afraid of what he might do if she kicks him out."

Oscar nodded and fell silent, his brow furrowed in thought, as it would be for the two months that followed, until the night he left.

"Hi Mom," Julio says. Lucina growls at Julio's voice so he has to say it again, this time loudly. He speaks to her in Spanish, though, to her constant dismay, the tip of his tongue is not quite as flexible as hers. His mother does not turn, yet he raises the sheet of paper into the air as if she has. "I need you to sign this."

This is a permission slip. What it declares is that, three days from now, on Thursday, Julio and his classmates, supplementary to their recent lessons on the American Civil War, are to board a school bus and travel to Monument Avenue. She will not understand it, and he doesn't need her to. He doesn't need her to know just how interested he is by the conflict, by the battles, by the causes, by the French assistance, the resolutions, or the fact that gallons of grey and blue blood still taint the farmlands. All he needs is her crooked signature.

"What?" Julio's mother asks, still turned. She cannot hear. Lucina's growling grows louder.

Julio raises his voice to repeat himself.

She turns to him briefly, but only to say, "What?" again.

Julio carefully steps closer, looking down so he does not step on the pups, or their chains. This, Julio thinks, this, Julio knows—the failure to communicate—is not the pups' fault. It is not Lucina's fault.

"I need you to sign this," he says for the third time. He takes his eyes off of his feet and looks at his mother, who is turning now, facing him, sidestepping her way back through the puppy shit as Lucina's growling swells. And then there is a sharp pain in Julio's right ankle. Then, the left. The pups are nibbling at him, their sharpest teeth not at all slowed by the fabric of his olive-colored pants. He tells them to stop. He moves his feet. He tells them once more, in English and in Spanish. And then, in one quick motion, he flings the pup from the top of his right foot. He watches the pup land on his shoulder, and is relieved to see him jump to his feet. But, seconds later, Julio is on the ground, holding his cheek. The blood will trickle to his neck when he stands, but not now, not when he is still coming to, when he can only make out his mother's, blurry face, the muffled sounds of his permission slip being shredded by puppy teeth.

If there were anything to be learned from the crowbar, Julio feels as if the lesson has been lost, replaced instead by an overwhelming desire to blame. He wants all of the blame to go to his mother. He wants it to rest squarely on her shoulders. But he knows that the placement would be wrong, that, as she has alluded to, at least some of it should go to the shoulders of the father he has met but does not remember. The Seed-Spreader, his mother has referred to him as. The man who stayed put, in the chaos of Mexico City, while his wife packed not only her one allotted suitcase, but the two for their young boys. The man that, no matter where his family was—San Diego, Omaha, Evanston, Richmond—no matter how displaced they felt, no matter how desperate they'd become, never sent so much as a peso.

"He was scared. That coward was scared that all American women are as fat as me," his mother has said before, to both Julio and Oscar. A statement spoken solemnly, regretfully. Infected with shame. "Fat and ugly, stupid women."

But Giuseppe deserves blame too, for the pain still swelling in and on Julio's cheek. He deserves blame for taking Lucina on that walk all those months back, for passing TACOS HERMANAS while Julio's mother, who had bummed a cigarette from Clarita, took a rare smoke break. For letting Lucina approach, and sniff, and somehow, someway, defying Giuseppe's myths, cuddle against the woman's thigh and lick the chicken juice from her knuckles. For persuading his mother to let him move in. For running his operation out of their only yard. For never caring about his mother unless he is rum-drunk. And, more importantly, for driving Oscar out. Poof, in one night, his seventeen-year-old brother gone, to Michigan, to asparagus picking and, "hopefully hay once summer hits," as he's mentioned in the letters he sends to Julio. They arrive once every couple of weeks, usually. Oscar sends them directly to Julio's school, so that neither Giuseppe nor their mother have the chance to read them, or steal the small amounts of cash Oscar bundles within. In one reply, Julio had mentioned that he'd been thinking of their father lately, trying to remember what he looked like. The next envelope from Oscar came within days. Rather than a letter, its contents consisted of a sketched portrait of their father. Bushy eyebrows, slick hair, low cheekbones. SEED-SPREADER! was written beneath the man's strong chin.

Julio has always looked up to Oscar. He's always appreciated Oscar. But, as much as he hates to think of it, he's beginning to understand that he, too, is deserving of blame. He may listen to Julio, he may talk with him and not at him, he may send letters and drawings, but the truth is that Oscar—not their mother, not Giuseppe—made the choice to leave. To abandon. To strip away the only armor his brother has ever known, and shove him into a battle he doesn't know how to fight.

Julio would give anything to receive a letter proving his thoughts wrong. Julio would give anything to tell any of them what he was doing, right now. I skipped school to take my own damn field trip, he'd say, or write. You hear me? All by myself, all for myself.

His face grows hot at the thought.

When two young women wearing matching red, white and blue T-shirts that shout, SAVE OUR UNION, hop onto the bus and raise their voices, Julio welcomes the distraction. They pass out fliers for some protest as the bus continues down the street. They shout that democracy today is a codeword for fascism. Passengers take the fliers, yes, but they return quickly to the urban decay outside of their window, blurred at this speed.

Julio turns his attention to the man splayed on the seat across the aisle. A damp green bandana is stretched from eyebrow to scalp, containing the frizz of his curly blonde hair. He possesses a beard of wizardly proportions, a dark blonde base with the occasional smudges of brown and grey. His eyes are shut. He snores lightly, and when the bus goes over a pothole, or jerks to a stop, the man's khaki combat boots swing. They just swing. Never to life, never to action. Just back and forth. What Julio finds most interesting, however, beyond the aforementioned, beyond the green army jacket, are the bullet casing tattoos stretching from knuckle to nail on each finger of his limp left hand. Within each casing are numbers, or letters, something rendered illegible either by Mother Nature or Father Time. But, even if they don't anymore, even if they have lost their luster, they once stood for something. They are a nod. An ode. A symbol. They, Julio thinks, once made a monument of his flesh.

###

Julio, standing in the center of Monument Avenue and Lombardy Avenue, gawks at a bronze J.E.B. Stuart. Stuart's saber is drawn. The horse he sits atop is rearing, readying for movement, following the order to take charge, to sprint toward and, eventually, through wave after wave of blue-coated men and cannonballs.

Julio is not joined by his classmates, or by anyone, really, the only passersby being a trio of tourists with heavy cameras strapped around their necks. The only thing, then, that throws Julio out of his stare, out of his desire to hop the fence and climb Stuart's granite pedestal, out of his desire to sit atop that horse and look down on Monument Avenue—its brick mansions, its elaborate churches—is the traffic. It is noon. Hungry Richmond workers honk at their inability to speed through a red light. Those at a stop gawk not at Stuart, but at Julio, at what he is convinced is his embarrassingly swollen cheek.

It's enough to make Julio move, to ignore the crosswalk and beeline through halted traffic to the sidewalk, and up the street, northwest, past large brick buildings, some with skinny chimneys at rest, others punctuated by pillars, until the sidewalk veers further north, beginning the traffic circle in which Robert E. Lee has been erected.

Including the pedestal, Lee and his horse are sixty feet above the grass beneath them. Lying on the lawn, enduring the mist, are what appear to be college students. Some toss around a football. Others close textbooks and opt to chat, sliding their pencils behind their ears. Leaning on the fence surrounding Lee are three people in raincoats, none of whom, as Julio can't help but doing as he proceeds northwest, stare at the tiered granite hoisting the statue and wonder if the tiers are meant to resemble steps. Steps that lead to Lee. Steps that lead to that rusting door beneath the statue, to Lee's heart, to Lee's soul. Because Lee, Julio thinks, is open. Lee is accommodating. And, though Julio someday soon wants to accept that invitation, now is not the time. He must heal before he does so.

He walks on, up the sidewalk, watching panting huskies and terriers brave the humidity and chase Frisbees across the grassy median. Of course, he thinks of Lucina, and wonders just how wrong Giuseppe has treated her, if any of his words can be taken as truth, if she really took down that Shepherd, or if those scars on his hand are actually from alley-way brawls over booze or women. For a moment, Julio pictures himself leashing Lucina and bringing her here, not to fight, not to squabble over a territory she has just claimed, but just to walk, to wade amongst the normal.

Just then, Julio feels it. He feels it, and then he sees it: a red-haired woman staring at him, at the wounds on his face. Julio squeezes his fingers around the backpack's straps. Sidesteps. Seeks space—

—which he finds it beneath Jefferson Davis. Davis, he has learned from Ms. Guiterrez, served as president of the Confederacy and, for this reason alone, he finds his monument to be fittingly extravagant—Davis himself, when compared to the entirety of the sculpture, is small, rendered nearly insubstantial by the size of the columns half-surrounding him. But Davis, as if recognizing that he alone weren't strong enough independently, has his right arm lifted and his hand open. "Rise, rise," it says to Julio. "Join." But join what? Julio wonders. THE ARMY OF THE CONFEDERATE STATES, as the inscription on the left-most column says? THE NAVY OF THE CONFEDERATE STATES? Join in numbers? Or, join the woman Davis seems to be lifting his arm toward—Miss Confederacy perched atop the Doric column in the center? Julio doesn't have an answer. But he walks, up the steps, back down, then around the monument, on the right side. He grazes his fingers over the

Latin phrase he does not understand, but reads aloud, PRO ARIS ET FOCI, before the approaching family of three are parallel, their conversation a series of whispers. The family stares. Julio returns to squeezing his backpack straps. He sidesteps until there is distance between them.

Julio walks past the heavily-trafficked statue of Stonewall Jackson, and thinks nothing else but that Jackson, other than facing a different direction, looks like he is mimicking Lee. Atop a horse. Proud. Staring down traffic. Eyes down, Julio moves past, moves forward, maneuvers around the crowd standing before the statue of Matthew Fontaine Maury, past the bronze earth and sea that weighs so heavily on the man's head. Off Julio goes, away from all, legs churning.

What causes him to stop, what completely and utterly confuses Julio, who had been led to believe that Monument Avenue was and is a place to commemorate those who stood up to what they thought was tyranny, is what he finds when he walks upon the Monument and Roseneath intersection. Because there, twelve feet tall, stands Arthur Ashe. Gazed upon by no one. He has seen the name before, on street signs, but he does not know who Arthur Ashe is, what he has accomplished. But he is black. And he looks angry. Angry, in a wrinkled tracksuit and rimmed glasses. The marble children standing beneath him appear to be excited, anxious even, for the tennis racquet Ashe is about to hit them with, or the books he is about to drop on their heads. Not a saber, Julio thinks. Books, and a tennis racket. Not a uniform; a tracksuit, and glasses.

###

"Julio," Oscar says. His hand is on Julio's shoulder, shaking him awake. "Julio, get up."

Julio rises and groggily looks at Oscar, at the clock, and across the room. It is 1:14am. His brother's bed is made. Not a pillow or blanket missing, or in disarray. And Oscar, Oscar is in jeans, a blue jacket and orange stocking cap. On his back is a bulging black backpack. In his eyes is a look of certainty, of conviction, that what he is about to say, that what he is about to do, is pure, absolute, and moral. It's this look that keeps Julio—who looks so young on this night, his hair much longer than what it will be on Monument Avenue, his own eyes just wet, fluttering blobs of miscomprehension—silent, eager to listen.

"I need your help," Oscar says. As far back as Julio can remember, Oscar, reliant on the self, has never uttered these words. Not to him, not to anyone. But those eyes. Once more, those eyes. Unblinking. Like stone. "I'm leaving, Julio, and I need your help."

"Okay," Julio says.

He gets out of bed, slips on a t-shirt and a pair of pajama pants and awaits instruction. Which he doesn't verbally receive. Oscar nods, then leads Julio out of their bedroom and alongside a sleeping Giuseppe on the living room sofa, stomach-down, face buried into the throw pillow. An empty pint of rum rests on the floor, flanked by an empty twenty-ounce Coke bottle. The way Oscar stares at Giuseppe as he and Julio pass says that what Oscar really wants to do is climb atop Giuseppe's back, grab handfuls of that curly black hair and bury his face into the pillow even further. He doesn't want a fight; he wants a kill. There's a rage in those eyes that Oscar is and has been struggling to contain. But he has: since the first night Giuseppe stayed; when he and Julio first heard their mother's headboard clapping against the wall, he has; he has since Giuseppe pulled them both aside one Saturday morning weeks after and said, "I'll be staying here some nights and you need to respect that."

The night Giuseppe moved in permanently, Oscar paced around he and Julio's bedroom. His hands were in his hair: "I don't want that drunk fucker here, Julio. I don't. I don't want his dog here, I don't want him on our couch, I don't want him eating our food. I don't want him in our mother's bed."

To which Julio replied, "Have you told Mom?"

"At least ten times. And you want to know what she says?" Oscar sat on Julio's bed then. "She said that I'm a burden. Said that she'd be primping herself up in some three-story hacienda if it weren't for me. Said Giuseppe would take her there. That I have no say."

Julio watched his brother shake his head and mumble something into his palms before asking, "Did she say that about me too?"

"No," Oscar said quickly. Too quickly. His eyes sold him out. Lies. How many had he told Julio over the years? He brought his hands back to his face. Spoke into them: "Of course not, Julio."

And now Oscar is sliding those same hands beneath their mother's mattress. He squats and, backpack still on, quietly pulls the mattress off of its box spring, off of its frame. Only then does he employ Julio's help, positioning him at the foot end of the mattress while he circles toward the headboard.

"What are you doing?" Julio whispers.

"Just lift," Oscar says.

"No." Julio won't. "Not until I know."

"I'm going to burn it," Oscar says. "And then I'm going to leave."

"Why? Why are you leaving?"

"You know why. And, once I make enough money, I'll help you leave, too." Oscar lifts his end of the mattress. "Now, will you help me or not?"

Most of Julio doesn't want to. He wants to let Oscar do this all on his own. He wants no part in the destruction, in the chaos, not when Julio will have to deal with the consequences of their actions entirely on his own, with Oscar long gone. He does not want to declare war; he wants to go back to bed. He doesn't want to leave. He wants to be in Richmond, in what throughout the past three years has become something of a home. He likes his school. He likes Ms. Guiterrez. He doesn't want to move again. Doesn't want another Omaha. Doesn't want another Evanston. He doesn't want another environment to shove him back into his shell, to kill the lights and lock the door. Because here, in Richmond, he can feel that shell starting to peel away. He knows street names. He knows which buses will take him where. He is certain that this city can play a part in the story of himself.

"What if he wakes up?"

"He won't. He's drunk."

Julio looks at the digital clock on his mother's nightstand. "She's going to be home soon," he tells Oscar. And she will, after the last-call wanderers of Richmond have been fed. She'll walk in with sore feet and hands, stinking of

TACOS HERMANAS chicken, makeup smeared, dark blue shirt damp with sweat.

Oscar still holds the mattress in his hands. "That's the point." He sighs. "Julio, please, just help, or get out of the way."

Moments later—after they, without so much as a nudged coaster or lamp, maneuver the mattress out of the bedroom, around Giuseppe and what will soon become his couch, through the front door and to the gravel driveway—Julio, though he wouldn't know how to explain it if asked, feels the fear wash away and something new take its place. He feels both sad and oddly satisfied. His stomach is full, his heart heavy. He feels with Oscar, not for Oscar. He, too, feels as if he is stepping eerily close to independence, to success, to accomplishment. It's pride. That's what he feels. Pride.

"Thank you," Oscar says to Julio in the driveway. He walks to Julio and gives him a hug. He even kisses his kid brother on the forehead. "I'll get you out of here. I promise. I will."

Julio nods. He wonders if he should cry here, in this moment. Because he doesn't feel the urge to. The hug was too brief to be final. Oscar will be back, he thinks. Oscar just needs a break. He'll be back soon. He will.

"Get inside," Oscar says. "You tell her that I did this. Hear me? You had nothing to do with it. Understand?"

Julio does. He says so. He nods. And then, as instructed, he goes inside, directly to what has in just one moment become solely his room. He opens the blinds. He watches Oscar douse the mattress with lighter fluid, then drop a lit match. In a moment, once he's deemed the fire before him satisfactory, Oscar will be gone, down the sidewalk and into darkness, reduced in Julio's life to this moment, to the handwritten letters that will follow. And, soon after, with the mattress still smoldering, his mother will park on the street and look around the neighborhood. She won't touch the mattress. But she'll shout. Oh yes, she'll shout, and she'll storm into the trailer, and Julio, still watching it all from his dark bedroom will jump into bed. He'll pull the covers over his face. He'll listen to her and Giuseppe yell. He'll hide. And he'll stay hidden like this for the months to come.

The rain has stopped. Brief as it was, the sun came out, but is now tucking itself beneath the quilt of night. With what light remains, Julio, looking down at the driveway, is convinced that he can still spot where the mattress turned to ash, where the flame blackened the gravel. But his eyes are deceiving him. Just as there are no cars in the driveway, there is no trace of the defiant moment that redefined Oscar. Outside of the squealing tires of a neighbor gunning his rusted Trans Am through an oft-ignored stop sign, the only sound is Lucina's growling. She cannot see Julio from the magnolia tree but she knows he is here. And she's known all along what he is capable of.

Julio walks to the edge of the doublewide and looks toward her. The pups are gone. Not one tumbles about, not one gnaws on a stick. Gone. To their new homes, their new lives. To cages. Julio grips his backpack straps and slouches while Lucina, despite the weight of the chain around her neck, stands erect beneath the magnolia, alert. Julio says nothing. Does not growl, like her, does not bark, does nothing but turn, walk across the lawn, up the two steps and into the house.

He walks through the living room—past the Giuseppe-stained sofa, past the empty bottles that have accumulated atop and beside the coffee table—to his bedroom. Days after Oscar burned her mattress, Julio's mother took it upon herself to drag the two twin-sized mattresses out of Julio's room and into her room, leaving Julio with only box springs. And this has gone unchanged, as has the placement of the box springs, Julio never having seen the point in stacking them, or rearranging them to maximize floor space, not when he's been sleeping on a pile of blankets, not when Oscar's return is inevitable. But, since yesterday, since the crowbar, since this afternoon, since Monument Avenue, since Arthur Ashe, that perceived inevitability is fading in Julio's mind. So much so that he flings his backpack at his brother's box spring. The backpack rolls to a halt while Julio is slinking to the floor. He touches his left cheek and grimaces, absorbs the pain. Runs his hand through his hair and listens to Lucina's chain scraping the magnolia's trunk.

And there is just too much, far too much colliding in Julio's brain. Oscar, his father, Giuseppe, the bus driver, Stonewall Jackson, Jefferson Davis quarreling, dancing, twisting, melding to one another, into something sharp, something much sharper than that crowbar. It is that sharp point that continues to puncture the good memories Julio has of his mother. The way she carried him up, down and across the streets of San Diego. The way she would smother his, and only his Omaha steaks with garlic butter before pan-frying them. How, in Evanston, she had Julio read his thin books to her before bed. How empowered that made him feel. How important. But they're oozing. The memories are oozing, binding, solidifying until Julio can find a semblance of the clarity he seeks. Two options, he thinks. There are two options, he knows, has known, will always know. Run, or—

The yellow beam of the old flashlight bobs as Julio walks quickly across the yard. Lucina rises, approaches, barks, lowers the barking to a growl, stretches her chain taut. Julio slows. He sets the flashlight on the grass so that Lucina's mismatched ears are swathed in yellow.

Julio, planted just feet outside of her reach, inches the curved end of the crowbar toward her. She sniffs the metal; her ears droop, from angry to anxious; she retreats. Julio advances. Steps his calves into the yellow light, then his knees and thighs.

He stares at Lucina and grows sad at the way her eyes are now shifting from the grass to the crowbar, from the crowbar to him. His eyes water. He begins to rethink what he has come out here to do, what he has for an hour now been considering. He ponders dropping the crowbar, stuffing his backpack with underwear and socks, with non-perishable food, and hitting the road, finding his way to Michigan. Leaving what he wants to become home without so much as a wave. Conceding.

"I'm sorry," Julio says. He can't. He won't. This is where he will stay. "I'm sorry," he says again, and wraps his free hand onto the crowbar, gripping it now as if it were a baseball bat.

Lucina cowers.

Julio swings.

Lucina cries, barks, bites.

Julio swings. Again. And again. And again, growling his way through the sounds of the crowbar connecting with Lucina's stomach, through the cries, through the cracking of ribs, through the physical surrender of what he knows is not his enemy.

Julio swings until Lucina is on her side. Blood has not yet reached air. She does not cry; she does not bark. Her tongue is on the grass. Her paws twitch.

Only when Julio catches his breath does he start sobbing. He buries his face into his shirt sleeve as he approaches her. He crouches. Pets her neck.

"I'm sorry," he says. "I'm sorry. I'm so sorry."

Moments later, Julio stands. He wipes his eyes, then regrips the crowbar. Rotates it in his hands so the pointed end is against Lucina's fur. Julio's hands are shaking.

"I'm so sorry," Julio sobs. "I'm so sorry."

Julio leans his weight onto the metal. The crowbar pierces Lucina's skin. Strikes bone, until it is redirected by Julio's pre-adolescent hands and shoved through the other side of Lucina, until Giuseppe's trophy has been anchored to the ground.

He lets go of the crowbar. Backs his way out of the yellow light. Studies what he has done. This is how he will leave her. He wonders if this is how they'll all remember him, in the dark, leaning against the magnolia tree.

JULIO:

CONQUEROR OF
THE CROWBAR

a *Strays Like Us* story by Garrett Francis

AUTHOR COMMENTARY

"Julio: Conqueror of the Crowbar" is a story from *Strays Like Us*, a collection of ten standalone stories exploring life as a kid growing up in America.

Via audio recordings on his website, author Garrett Francis gives readers a peek behind each of these short stories.

If you're interested in learning more about the thoughts and processes that went into "Julio: Conqueror of the Crowbar" visit garrettfrancis.substack.com/p/commentary-julio-crowbar-short-story.

ABOUT THE AUTHOR

Garrett Francis is the author of the novel *And in the Dark They Are Born* and the short story collection *Strays Like Us*. He grew up on a small farm in Michigan and earned his B.A. in Creative Writing from Grand Valley State University.

In 2012, Garrett co-founded *Squalorly,* a digital literary journal of the Midwest and served as its nonfiction editor until 2014.

In 2016, founded Orson's Publishing in 2016, a micro press and served as the press's sole editor (and designer, and publicist, among other roles) until its closure in 2020, publishing four book-length works by new and emerging authors.

He also founded *Orson's Review* in 2017, a digital literary journal that served as a companion to its parent press, publishing fiction, creative nonfiction, poetry and photography. He served as the sole editor of *Orson's Review* as well, and is proud to have helped bring the work of over 70 international contributors to life.

Today, Garrett lives in Seattle, Washington with his family. Short works of his have been published in literary journals like *Midwestern Gothic, Barely South Review, Whiskeypaper* and *Monkeybicycle.* He keeps a day job and when he isn't working or writing, he tries to be outside as much as he can—camping, hiking, kayaking, and just generally wandering.

###

Use the QR code below to subscribe to Garrett Francis's newsletter, where you'll receive exclusive access to his thoughtful fiction, creative nonfiction, screenplays, commentary and more.